Silky the Fairy enters the Land of Mine-All-Mine from the Faraway Tree looking for adventure. She has visited many Lands in search of fun and excitement. But when she meets Talon the evil Troll she soon finds that her Enchanted World is turned upside down.

To rescue the Talismans that have been lost from the Faraway Tree, Silky will need some help, and fast! Luckily she can rely on her best fairy friends to help her in her task. With the special talents of Melody, Petal, Pinx and Bizzy, Silky must save the Lands of the Enchanted World. But will the fairies succeed or will Talon get his evil way?

EGMONT

We bring stories to life

Melody and the Gemini Locket
Published in Great Britain 2009
by Egmont UK Limited
239 Kensington High Street, London W8 6SA

Text and illustrations
ENID BLYTON® ENID BLYTON'S ENCHANTED
WORLD™ Copyright © 2009 Chorion Rights Limited.
All rights reserved.

Text by Elise Allen
Illustrations by Dynamo

ISBN 978 1 4052 4675 0

1 3 5 7 9 10 8 6 4 2

A CIP catalogue record for this title is available from the British
Library

Printed and bound in Great Britain by the CPI Group

Enid Blyton's ENCHANTED WORLD

Melody and the Gemini Locket

By Elise Allen

EGMONT

Meet the Faraway Fairies

Favourite Colour – Yellow. It's a beautiful colour that reminds me of sunshine and happiness.

Talent – Light. I can release rays of energy to light up a room or, if I really try hard, I can use it to break out of tight situations. The only problem is that when I lose my temper I can have a 'flash attack' which is really embarrassing because my friends find it funny.

Favourite Activity – Exploring. I love an adventure, even when it gets me into trouble. I never get tired of visiting new places and meeting new people.

Favourite Colour – Blue. The colour of the sea and the sky. I love every shade from aquamarine to midnight blue.

Talent – As well as being a musician I can also transform into other objects. I like to do it for fun, but it also comes in useful if there's a spot of bother.

Favourite Activity – Singing and dancing. I can do it all day and never get tired.

Favourite Colour – Green. It's the colour of life. All my best plant friends are one shade of green or another.

Talent – I can speak to the animals and plants of the Enchanted World . . . not to mention the ones in the Faraway Tree.

Favourite Activity – I love to sit peacefully and listen to the constant chatter of all creatures, both big and small.

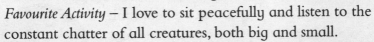

Favourite Colour – Pink. What other colour would it be? Pink is simply the best colour there is.

Talent – Apart from being a supreme fashion designer, I can also become invisible. It helps me to escape from my screaming fashion fans!

Favourite Activity – Designing. Give me some fabrics and I'll make you something fabulous. Remember – If it's not by Pinx . . . your makeover stinks!

Favourite Colour – Orange. It's the most fun colour of all. It's just bursting with life!

Talent – Being a magician of course. Although I have been known to make the odd Basic Bizzy Blunder with my spells.

Favourite Activity – Baking Brilliant Blueberry Buns and Marvellous Magical Muffins. There is always time to bake a tasty cake to show your friends that you care.

www.blyton.com/enchantedworld

Contents

Introduction

Tucked away among the thickets, groves and forests of our Earth is a special wood. An Enchanted Wood, where the trees grow taller, the branches grow stronger and the leaves grow denser than anywhere else. Search hard enough within this Enchanted Wood, and you'll find one tree that towers above all the others. This is the Faraway Tree, and it is very special. It is home to magical creatures like elves and fairies, even a dragon. But the most magical thing about this very magical Tree? It is the sole doorway to the Lands of the Enchanted World.

Most of the time, the Lands of the Enchanted World simply float along, unattached to anything.

But at one time or another, they each come to rest at the top of the Faraway Tree. And if you're lucky enough to be in the Tree at the time, you can climb to its very top, scramble up the long Ladder extending from its tallest branch, push through the clouds and step into that Land.

Of course, there's no telling when a Land will come to the Faraway Tree, or how long it will remain. A Land might stay for months, or be gone within the hour. And if you haven't made it back down the Ladder and into the Faraway Tree before the Land floats away, you could be stuck for a very long time. This is scary even in the most wonderful of Lands, like the Land of Perfect Birthday Parties. But if you get caught in a place like the Land of Ravenous Toothy Beasts, the situation is absolutely terrifying. Yet even though exploring the Lands has its perils, it's also exhilarating, which is why creatures from all over the Enchanted World (and the occasional visiting human) come to live in the Faraway Tree so they can travel from Land to Land.

Of course, not everyone explores the Lands for pleasure alone. In fact, five fairies have been asked to do so for the ultimate cause: to save the life of the Faraway Tree and make sure the doorway to the Enchanted World remains open. These are their stories . . .

Chapter One
Coming Unstuck

'NO! NO NO NO NO *NO!*'
Pinx's screams echoed throughout
the Faraway Fairies' treehouse. Unable to
keep her fury to herself, she flew down to the
main room.

'There is *sap* in my *wardrobe*!' she wailed.
'*SAP*! My taffetellas, satinellas and bubbloons
are all stuck together into one giant fashion
mess!'

Bizzy, meanwhile, bustled away in the
kitchen, tending to countless vats of boiling
sap spread over ten different oven tops, nine of
which she had magicked up for just this
occasion.

'I know!' she agreed with Pinx. 'We're
Swimming in a Sea of Sappy Stickiness! I'm

trying to make syrup with it, but there's just too much of it!'

'It's even in my hair.' cried Silky from the main room, as Melody tried to wrestle a comb through Silky's tresses. 'OW!'

'Sorry, Silky,' Melody winced. 'The sap is just sticking it together in one giant knot.'

'So much for gratitude,' Pinx huffed, rubbing her hands to try and remove the sappy stickiness. 'We work our wings off to rescue Talismans and save the Tree and this is

how it repays us.'

'It's not the Tree's fault,' Silky replied, cringing as Melody tugged on her tangled hair. 'The Talismans are its life force. Until they're all back in the Vault, the Tree can't help but have problems sometimes.'

'CAW!'

Petal's raven friend zipped into the room, flapping his left wing wildly as he tried to dislodge something from it.

Melody looked up. 'The Eternal Bloom!' she gasped.

'Oh, goodness!' cried the Bloom as the raven shook her about. 'Good birdie . . . nice birdie.' When trying to soothe the bird didn't work, she screamed out, 'PETAAAAAALLLL!'

'I'm coming!' cried Petal, zooming after the frightened Bloom. 'It's OK. The raven isn't trying to hurt you; he's just frightened.'

'You think *he's* frightened!' wailed the Bloom.

Knowing the Eternal Bloom – a *Talisman* – was in real danger, Silky, Melody, Bizzy and Pinx immediately joined Petal's rescue attempt.

'What happened?' Bizzy asked, lunging for the bird as it swiftly darted away.

'The sap,' Petal huffed. 'It stuck the Bloom to the raven's wing.'

'Here she comes!' Pinx cried. 'I'll get her!'

As the raven approached, Pinx threw herself at the panicking bird, but all she got was a loud squawk in her ear and a handful of feathers as he dodged her grasp. Even with all five fairies trying their best, the raven was simply impossible to catch. He was so bothered and confused by the added weight on his wing that he wouldn't even listen to Petal's attempts to comfort him. He zipped and zoomed and zigged and zagged around, always remaining just out of the fairies' reach.

Finally, the raven flew to the very centre of

the room, in the middle of all the fairies.

'I've got him!' Pinx, Petal, Melody, Bizzy and Silky all cried at once, leaping towards him . . .

. . . SPLOOSH!

A waterfall of soapy old wash-water poured through the ceiling, drenching the five fairies, the raven and the Bloom.

'URGH!' cried Silky, disgusted.

'We're Swimming in a Soup of Soiled Suds!' Bizzy added, equally unhappy.

'And it's all over *everything*!' Petal moaned, finally easing the Bloom off the raven's wing and releasing the bird.

'DAME WASHALOT!' Pinx exploded, flying to the nearest window to scream up to their neighbour. 'PLEASE! YOU *MUST* BE MORE CAREFUL ABOUT WHERE YOU SPILL YOUR WASH-WATER!'

A kindly voice lilted back down to her. 'Is that you, Pinx, dear?' Dame Washalot asked.

'Lovely to hear from you, but I can't chat now. Awfully busy with all this sap, you know. *Lots* of extra washing.'

This was, of course, precisely the problem. Dame Washalot did the washing for everyone in the Faraway Tree and with all the leaking sap there was quite a lot more laundry for her to do than usual. So much more, in fact, that she had to set up several extra wash bowls, one of which splashed into the fairies' main room every time she tipped out the dirty water. The fairies tried again and again to explain this to Dame Washalot, but she was so caught up in her massive workload that she didn't seem to understand.

'But Dame Washalot . . .' Pinx began. Then she heard a happy humming, which meant Dame Washalot was back to her scrubbing and couldn't hear a thing. 'This is *impossible*!' Pinx screamed to the other fairies in frustration. 'The sap alone is bad enough, but

*** 9 ***

a filthy waterfall raining down on us every . . .'

Pinx stopped in her tracks and stared at Melody, stunned. 'Are you *laughing*?' she asked her friend in disbelief.

'It *is* awfully funny,' Melody tittered. 'I mean, look at us!'

'It's not funny, it's infuriating!' Pinx retorted. 'How come you're not as upset as the rest of us?'

Melody shrugged. 'I just don't see the purpose in it, I guess. It's not like getting angry will change anything, so why bother?'

'*Why bother?*' Pinx echoed. 'It's not about "bothering"; it's about *feeling*! Don't you ever feel anything but blissfully happy?'

'Pinx . . .' Silky warned.

'No, I'm serious,' Pinx insisted, then turned back to Melody. 'I don't think I've ever seen you really angry. Why is that?'

'I do get angry,' Melody insisted. 'I just choose to let it go. I feel better when I don't let my emotions run away with me.'

'Well, that's just silly,' Pinx declared. 'You can't "choose" what you feel. You either feel something or you don't.'

'*I* feel a Talisman mission about to start,' said a familiar voice, and the fairies turned towards the front door.

'Witch Whisper!' they cried, flying over to surround both her and Cluecatcher, who had come to visit too.

Cluecatcher had uncanny senses, which came as no surprise to anyone who saw him. He had no less than four pairs of eyes, huge ears that stood to attention, sensitive to the slightest sound, and a massive nose that stretched the entire length of his face. He always seemed focused on the world around him, ready to pick up any change – but not today. Today he kept squinting his eight eyes, scrunching up his nose, and shaking his head from side to side as if trying to dislodge something from his ears.

'I apologise for barging in,' Witch Whisper said to the fairies, 'but we may have lost some time. There's a new Land at the top of the Tree, although we're not quite sure how long it's been there.'

'It's the sap,' Cluecatcher explained, tilting his right ear down to the floor and hopping up and down to clear it. 'It gets in my ears and my nose. They've been clogged for days. But I've finally got them clean enough to pick up the new Land.'

Cluecatcher leaned back his enormous head and gave a mighty – if somewhat muffled – sniff. Then he nodded. 'Yes, I'm sure of it. It's the Land of Doubles.'

'The Land of Doubles?' Silky and Petal asked in unison. They looked at each other and laughed.

'The Land of Doubles is quite unusual,' said Witch Whisper. 'It formed around an enchanted mirror, so everyone and everything there is

born or grows with a double, and all those
doubles are tied to the Land. When we made
the Talismans, we took the smallest segment of
that mirror, divided it in two and placed the
pieces into a necklace charm to make the
Gemini Locket.'

'Let me guess,' said Pinx. 'It's amazingly

beautiful and powerful and no one in the Land will ever want to give it up.'

'Actually, Pinx, it's a very simple necklace,' Witch Whisper noted with a smile. 'Almost certainly too plain to make it into your wardrobe, but beautiful nonetheless. Speaking of which . . .' Witch Whisper's smile grew, taking in the fairies' drenched and soapy state. 'You might need a little help if you're going to get to the Land before it moves away from the Tree.'

With a quick spell, she got rid of the sap and dirty wash-water covering the group, leaving them clean and dry.

'This is *great*!' Pinx crowed, admiring her freshly restored outfit. Then she turned to Witch Whisper eagerly. 'Hey, can we go up to my wardrobe and de-sap the rest of my clothes? It'll only take a couple of minutes.'

'Pinx,' Silky cajoled her – it was really time to leave.

But Witch Whisper didn't seem bothered. 'They're already done,' she said with a twinkle in her eye.

'YES!' Pinx cheered, then zipped out of the treehouse and led the way to the Ladder, the other fairies following right behind her.

'The Land of Doubles . . .' Petal mused as they flew. 'I wonder what it would be like to have a double. I imagine it would be lovely.'

'I almost have a double, remember?' Bizzy noted. 'My sister, Berry. We look virtually identical and, believe me, it's not lovely at all.'

'I would hate to have a double,' Pinx said. 'Too much competition.'

Silky agreed. 'I'm hard enough on myself as it is. Having another me there to point out all my mistakes? No, thank you.'

Melody, however, shook her head, smiling. 'I think a double would be wonderful. Imagine – a friend who knows you inside out, who understands your every hope and dream.

She'd be the perfect companion — even when you just wanted to be by yourself!'

They all laughed at that, and the sound of their glee echoed down the Ladder as they pushed through the cloud at the top and climbed into the Land of Doubles.

Chapter Two
The Fastest Mission Yet?

Even though they knew it was the Land of Doubles, the fairies couldn't help but rub their eyes as they took in the view before them. They had emerged from the Ladder into a beautiful meadow, spread wide with thick, lush, knee-high grass and tall, colourful flowers. Full oaks, elms and maples dotted the landscape, their leaves dappled in all shades of green. Woodland creatures were everywhere, the smaller ones hidden by the grass until they scrambled on to a rock, branch or stump. Squirrels, rabbits, deer and birds of all kinds happily made their home in the meadow, and all seemed perfectly peaceful and serene.

Peaceful, serene — and doubled.

Every tree, every rock, every animal had an

exact duplicate. Twin rabbits hopped across a
knoll, twin deer perked up their heads at the
sound of the fairies' footsteps and twin maples
shaded twin boulders from the glare of the
twin suns in the sky.

'Oh!' gasped Silky, jumping back as two
identical, fuzzy squirrel heads popped up
from side-by-side holes in a tree, right in front
of her.

'Aaah,' cooed Melody. 'They're exactly alike.'

'Except they're not,' said Petal, cocking her head to observe the squirrels. 'Look.'

Melody had approached the tree and held out a hand to the squirrels. One crawled right into her palm and up her arm as if to playfully say hello, then chirped with delight as Melody scratched behind his ear. The other

squirrel cowered in its hole at the sight of the fairies and refused to come back up.

'They look alike, but they have different personalities,' Bizzy realised.

Petal nodded. 'And it's not just the animals. See those two oak trees? One of them wants to race to see who can change their leaf colours faster, and the other says it hates to compete. It's interesting.'

'Yeah,' Pinx agreed with a smirk. 'Shame we won't be around to explore for much longer. Look.' She pointed to Silky's crystal necklace, which they all noticed was glowing a bright red.

'The Talisman!' Silky gasped. 'It must be right here!'

Melody returned her squirrel friend to his tree and the five fairies took to the air to scan the area.

Within seconds, Pinx saw it. There, just dangling from the highest branches of a tall maple was the Gemini Locket.

Silky, Bizzy, Petal, Melody and Pinx all gathered in the canopy of the maple's leaves to get a closer look. It was very plain, just as Witch Whisper had said: a thin gold chain from which dangled a golden oval pendant decorated around its edge in raised gold filigree.

'I don't understand,' Bizzy said. 'What's a Talisman doing hanging from a tree in the middle of nowhere?'

'It actually makes sense,' Silky said. 'When Witch Whisper magicked the Talismans away from Talon, she just sent them to their original Lands, not to anywhere specific within those Lands. This

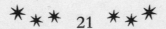

one must have ended up here where no one found it.'

'Would you like to do the honours?' Pinx asked Silky, gesturing to the Locket. Silky reached out and grabbed it, but the minute her fingers clasped the chain, the fairies heard a loud POP . . .

. . . and saw Talon appear right next to the maple tree, having magicked himself into the Land. Not realising how close he was to the Talisman, he flashed his angry eyes over the meadow, wondering where to start his search.

'*Hurry!*' Petal whisper-hissed to the fairies, hoping they could slip away before Talon saw them.

But it was too late. Talon looked up and immediately fixed on the Locket in Silky's hands.

'Fly away!' Silky cried, but the fairies never had the chance. With a wicked grin, Talon grabbed the maple tree and recited a spell in Trollish. His crystal flashed and the tree's branches sprang to life, reaching out like arms to grab all five of the fairies – and tickle them!

It certainly wasn't the attack the fairies were expecting, but it was effective. The tickling left them in fits: they screamed, they laughed, they wriggled – and they couldn't think clearly enough to use their powers at all.

Grinning proudly, Talon enchanted the trunk of the tree to become stairs so he could walk up and stand over Silky.

'NO!' she cried, but she was helpless to do anything but laugh and squirm as Talon plucked the Locket from her grasp.

'Thank you, Silky,' Talon smiled, 'for making this so wonderfully easy for me.'

But before Talon could recite the spell that would take him back home, an orange-ponytailed blur zipped by, grabbed the Locket from Talon and raced away.

'WHAT?' Talon roared. He stared down at his hands in shock then glared after the fairy who had stolen his prize. 'Melody,' he growled. 'How did you —?'

'I'm not ticklish, Talon!' Melody called back, not even looking over her shoulder as she gritted her teeth and made a mad dash for the Ladder.

Talon sneered. There was no way he was letting another Talisman slip away. He leaped off the maple tree and on to a rock, which he enchanted to rocket him towards Melody.

It wasn't long before he caught up with her. With a mighty snarl, he leaped off the rock and tackled her, forcing them both to the ground. Pinned beneath Talon, Melody could see nothing but the hideous Troll's face.

'You may not be ticklish, little fairy,' Talon hissed, the hot stink of his breath clouding her senses, 'but you're certainly not immune to magic.' He quickly spat out a spell in Trollish and his crystal flashed.

Thinking quickly, Melody transformed into

a brightly polished tuba with the Gemini Locket held tightly in its coils. Talon's spell bounced harmlessly off the tuba's bright surface before Melody sounded a single loud long note.

The noise was too much for Talon to bear and he staggered back, clutching his ears. Seizing her chance to escape, Melody turned back into herself and raced for the Ladder, but she wasn't fast enough. Talon dived at her, knocking her sideways towards the tickling tree. One of the flailing branches caught her wing tip, tearing it painfully. Melody gasped, dropping the Locket into the tall grass.

But she recovered quickly and both she and Talon dropped to the ground in search of the Locket. They spotted it at the same moment. It had popped open, and both Talon and Melody lunged for it, each grabbing one side of the open charm and pulling for dear life.

SNAP!

The Locket came apart, throwing both
Talon and Melody violently backwards on to

the grass. As it broke, a huge flash of blinding
light burst from inside it, enveloping both the
fairy and the Troll.

Though Silky, Bizzy, Petal and Pinx had
tried to watch what was happening, they had
been completely at the mercy of the tickling

tree. Yet the branches had stopped when the light flashed, and now the fairies raced to help Melody — only to find both their friend and Talon lying on the ground, unconscious.

Chapter Three
Melody and Mel

'MELODY!' the fairies cried, racing towards her. Talon, meanwhile, began to stir and rise, but the fairies were too focused on their friend to even notice. Petal leaned down over her, looking closely for signs of life.

'She's breathing,' Petal said, relieved. 'She's OK, just unconscious.'

Behind them, a wickedly triumphant growl made Pinx, Petal, Silky and Bizzy spin round.

It was Talon, on his feet and holding the Gemini Locket high above his head in a tightly clenched fist. 'You lose this time, fairies! Get used to the feeling!' He closed his eyes and recited a spell in Trollish just as another figure that looked exactly like Talon rose and pounced on him.

The crystal flashed and they both disappeared.

Silky, Petal, Bizzy and Pinx could only stare, agape. Bizzy was the first to speak, her voice small and stunned.

'We failed,' she said. 'Talon took the Talisman.'

The other fairies had no response. It was terrible, but true. For the first time ever, they had failed a mission. The Land of Doubles would now belong to Talon and the Faraway Tree had forever lost part of its life force. The idea was too awful to bear, but Silky knew they couldn't dwell on it. Not now.

'We'll tell Witch Whisper,' Silky declared. 'Let's make sure Melody's OK and we'll go.' Yet even as she said it, something was nagging at her. Something Witch Whisper had said about doubles that could change this situation entirely.

But Silky couldn't think about that now;

she was too worried about Melody. She, Pinx and Bizzy watched as Petal again bent over their friend. Gently, Petal brushed Melody's cheek and Melody finally started to stir just the littlest bit.

'Honestly, it's not like she's made of glass,' came a voice. 'Give her a good shake. Throw cold water in her face. That'd work for me.'

The voice sounded just like Melody's. Immediately, Pinx, Petal, Bizzy and Silky looked up to find its source, only to see a fairy who looked just like their friend. The fairy getting to her feet just a couple of metres beyond Melody wore the same blue leotard and the same pink tutu. She had the same orange ponytail and green eyes too. But her words were much more knowing than Melody's and those eyes held an impish delight that wasn't Melody's at all.

'Witch Whisper said the Gemini Locket was made from the same mirror used to make all the doubles in this Land,' Petal said softly, not taking her eyes off the amazing sight of Melody's twin. 'You don't suppose that this is —'

'My double!' Melody gasped as she rose and came face to face with her twin.

She reached out for a hug, but her double stepped back at the last minute, making Melody lose her balance and stumble forwards.

'Hey, we've only just met. Take it easy,' said the Melody lookalike. Then she grimaced and reached up, feeling the back of her head. 'What's up with this ponytail? It's so tight it feels like it's pulling my face off!'

'What do you mean?' Melody asked. 'I always wear a ponytail.'

'*I* don't,' the other Melody retorted. She pulled out the elastic band, shaking her head so her hair flowed wild and free down her back. '*Much* better. How do I look?'

'Messy!' Melody cried. 'That's not how a Twinkletune wears her hair!'

'I like it,' the new Melody shrugged. 'So, what do we call ourselves?'

'My name – *our* name is Melody.'

'Melody . . .' The other Melody rolled the name on her tongue a moment, then shook her head. 'Nope. That's far too sweet for me. I want to be Mel.'

'*Mel?*' Melody echoed, aghast.

'Mel,' Pinx said, grinning. 'I like that.'

'It's cool, isn't it?' Mel said. She turned to

Pinx, taking her in for the first time, and her eyes grew wider. 'I love your outfit.'

'It's my own design,' Pinx crowed happily, and twirled so Mel could admire it from every angle.

'Brilliant!' Mel declared, then leaned closer to Pinx. 'Think you can do anything about this monstrosity I'm wearing? It's *hideous*.'

'Hideous!' Melody screeched. 'I'm wearing the same outfit!'

Pinx didn't seem to notice Melody's outburst. She was too busy assuring Mel she could do wonders with her outfit, and was already making little folds and adjustments to the leotard and skirt.

Silky, Bizzy and Petal looked on in amazement.

'Unbelievable,' Silky declared after a moment.

'Is she Melody's double, or Pinx's?' Bizzy joked.

Petal just shook her head, too surprised and amused to speak.

'Oh, hey! Look at this!' Mel bent down to pick up a shiny gold object on the ground that had caught her eye. It was a simple oval attached to a piece of chain. One side was gold with a filigree edge, the other side held a tiny piece of mirror.

'It's half of the Gemini Locket!' Silky gasped.

'Yes!' Melody realised. 'Talon and I ripped it apart. That must be what made my double!'

'Mel,' Mel corrected her.

'*Mel*,' Melody grudgingly repeated.

'And Talon's double too,' Petal noted. 'We saw it grab Talon before he disappeared.'

'So if Talon only has half the Locket, the mission isn't over!' Bizzy cried, elated.

'Exactly. He'll be back for the other half, which is when we can get *his* half,' Silky said.

'*If* he brings it back. What if he leaves the

other half wherever he lives?' Petal worried.

'That's it!' Silky had finally remembered what had been bothering her. 'Remember what Witch Whisper said? Doubles here are tied to the Land. So if Talon is now a double, he *can't* get back to where he lives. Wherever the two of them disappeared to, it must be somewhere in the Land!'

'Well, we won't be using your crystal to find them,' Pinx noted. 'I don't think it cares much for a broken Talisman.'

The fairies followed Pinx's gaze. Silky's crystal necklace had turned a muddy purple-black. It would be useless on this mission until the Talisman was whole.

'So, what do we do now?' Mel asked. 'Just wait here for the Troll?'

'*We?*' Melody asked uncomfortably.

'We,' Mel repeated. 'Seems I'm one of you lot now, aren't I? And I'm certainly up for a bit of an adventure. Though I'd rather you

held on to this. I'd hate to be the one to let it slip from my hands.' Mel handed the Locket half to Silky, who put it in her pocket. 'So,' Mel's dancing eyes met Silky's. 'Am I in?'

Silky smiled. Mel had a mischievous energy that was quite impossible to resist. 'Of course you're in!' she said.

'Brilliant!' Pinx cried, wrapping her new best friend Mel in a hug.

'Right . . . brilliant,' Melody echoed
through a forced smile.

'I can hear something,' Bizzy suddenly said,
and, as everyone listened closely, they heard it
too: peals of laughter.

Curious, the six fairies began to fly towards
the sound, but both Mel and Melody quickly
landed again.

'OW!' they cried out in pain, looking at

each other curiously.

'What happened?' Petal asked.

'It's my wing,' Melody said. 'I caught it on the tree just before the Locket snapped, but I thought it was OK . . . until I tried to fly.'

'So you gave me a broken wing!' Mel complained.

'It's not like I did it on purpose!' Melody protested.

But before either she or Mel could say anything else, Petal chimed in, 'It's fine; we're all happy to walk.'

So the fairies followed the sounds of laughter on foot to a far copse of trees. Peeking through the leaves, they saw a small village filled with several pairs of doubles, all moving in tandem.

'They're dancing!' Melody exclaimed, instantly charmed. 'We should talk to them.'

Melody started towards the village, but Mel held her back. 'We *shouldn't* talk to them. We don't know if they're friendly.'

Melody looked at her double, completely stunned. 'But . . . they're dancing. And it's a joyful dance. Look!'

Mel wouldn't look. 'I don't care if it's the most joyful dance in the world, it doesn't mean they're *friendly*.'

'Yes! Finally a Twinkletune who makes sense!' Pinx cried. Indignant, Melody turned red.

'Actually, I agree with Melody,' Silky said. She had been watching the dancers, and they did seem rather harmless. Why not get to know them while they waited for Talon to show up with his half of the Gemini Locket? 'Let's say hello, but not all at once. Maybe just Melody first. If they like dancing, perhaps watching her will warm them up for visitors.'

'Whoa, whoa, whoa!' Mel objected. 'If that's the plan, I choose me. I'm a dancer too, you know, and I can certainly impress the villagers as much as Melody can.'

'I wasn't planning to *impress* them,' Melody protested. 'I'll just do a few steps, introduce myself, say hello . . .'

But Mel didn't let Melody finish her sentence. 'OK, then – I'm off!' she cried, and did a leaping run into the middle of the group of villagers. 'Hey everyone, look at meee!'

Chapter Four
Stay or Go

The villagers were in awe. They stared as Mel executed a string of amazingly intricate moves. She even threw in a decouple twirliette, which no one but Melody had ever accomplished before.

From their hiding place in the bushes, Pinx grinned. 'She's really good.'

The other fairies threw her a disapproving look.

'What?' Pinx asked, then reconsidered. 'OK, yes, she shouldn't have just jumped into the village like that ... but she's really good!'

Mel finished with a flourish and shouted, 'So, what do you think? Did you love it?'

The villagers stared up at her for one last moment – then scattered into their huts and

slammed the doors, bolting them shut.

'Oh, come *on*!' Mel cried. 'That was spectacular!' When the villagers didn't stir, she threw her arms in the air and called out to the fairies, 'You may as well come out. It's just us now. Everyone else seems to be locked away.'

'I think they're a little frightened,' Melody said gently as she and the other fairies emerged from behind the trees. 'I mean, we don't know if they've even seen fairies before and you might have come on the teensiest bit strong . . .'

'Are you trying to say you would have done things better?' Mel asked. 'Because if you are, go ahead and say it, don't pussyfoot around.'

The direct challenge made Melody blush. 'What? No! I'm not saying that at all! I just –'

'Um, Mel. Melody.' Bizzy interrupted them. 'I think we have company.'

Mel and Melody turned to see that all the villagers had emerged from their huts and gathered to stare at the fairy pair. Two of the villagers stood in front of the others. They were slightly shorter than Mel and Melody and had matching manes of maroon curls. One of them wore an open, excited grin and the other looked timidly at her feet, casting the occasional shy smile their way.

'Where are your doubles?' they asked Silky, Pinx, Bizzy and Petal in unison. One asked confidently, while the other whispered the question.

'We don't have doubles.' Silky glanced at her fellow fairies. 'We're just visiting, actually.'

The grinning villager seemed happy with this answer.

'I see. Sorry we ran off before; we didn't realise. I'm Cassie, and this is my double, Polly.' She looked at Melody and Mel. 'We were all just practising for the Dance of the Doubles. Want to join us?'

'Sure!' said Melody, quite taken by Cassie's enthusiasm.

'How?' asked Mel. 'We don't *know* the Dance of the Doubles.'

Melody smiled to try and make up for Mel's contrariness. 'No, but I'm sure we could follow their lead.'

This was the wrong thing to say. Cassie, Polly and the rest of the villagers suddenly grew ashen. 'You mean you don't have parts in the Dance of the Doubles?' Cassie asked.

'We're kind of new to the whole doubles

thing,' Melody admitted, hoping her disappointment about her particular double wasn't horribly obvious.

'Then you have to get to Geminopolis, right away!' Cassie exclaimed. 'The Dance of the Doubles is at sunset tonight, and every pair of doubles has to do their assigned part!'

'It's only morning,' Pinx said. 'We're aiming to be gone by sunset.'

'I hope you are,' Cassie said worriedly. 'But if there's even the slightest chance you're staying, please, you must go to Geminopolis.'

'I don't understand. Why is it so important for them to get a part in the Dance of the Doubles?' Petal asked.

'The annual Dance of the Doubles is how this Land gets its energy. Every year, all the doubles come together and dance. That's what powers the Land for another year,' Cassie explained.

'How far away is Geminopolis? Can you

take us there?' Melody asked.

Cassie shook her head, but seemed much happier now that Melody was considering the trip. 'We have to stay and practise, but it's very simple. All you have to do is follow The Way.' She pointed to a path just behind the village, covered in black-and-white checkerboard tiles. 'It winds through the Land of Doubles. Follow it and you'll get to Geminopolis and the Ministers of Motion. They'll give you your assignment.'

'We'll do it,' Silky declared, just as Pinx said, 'No thanks; we're not interested.'

Silky and Pinx looked at each other a moment, then turned back to Cassie and Polly. 'Excuse us,' they said as one.

As the villagers nervously huddled together awaiting the final decision, the fairies huddled together for a chat.

'Why wouldn't we go and get the dance assignment?' Silky asked Pinx.

'I don't know . . . maybe because we have more important things to do, like get the other half of the Gemini Locket and save the Enchanted World.' Pinx retorted.

'But we can't do that without Talon, and he could be anywhere,' Melody noted. 'Plus, the Dance of the Doubles seems really important to the villagers. I agree with Silky; I say we go.'

'Why? We're not *from* this Land, so the Dance of the Doubles has nothing to do with us,' Mel countered. 'Besides, this place is full of doubles – one pair not doing the Dance won't hurt it.'

'We don't know that,' Petal said. 'You haven't seen what we have, Mel. Some of these Lands work in ways we'd never imagined possible.'

'So if there's even a chance that we'll be here at sunset, and that you and Melody dancing will help the Land, we *have* to get your assignment,' Silky concluded.

'But what about Talon?' Bizzy asked. 'If he comes back here looking for us, we'll want to be here.'

'Talon has always been very good at finding us,' Silky countered. 'And he needs our half of the Talisman as much as we need his. I don't think we have to worry.'

'Looks like we're split three–three,' Mel grinned. 'What do we usually do in a tie?'

'We usually don't have six fairies, we have

five,' Melody muttered under her breath, but so softly that no one heard her.

'I know!' Bizzy declared, 'we'll have a Tried and Tested Traditional Tie-Breaker. We'll flip a coin!' With a few magic words and a wave of her wand, she magicked up a coin, then asked Silky to call it.

'Heads,' Silky said.

'Got it,' Bizzy confirmed. Heads we follow The Way, tails we stay here.' Bizzy tossed the coin into the air and all the fairies watched it spin. It landed on the ground and they all bent down to look.

'It's heads!' Silky cried happily, then turned back to the villagers. 'Cassie, I'm happy to say we're going to Geminopolis to see the Ministers of Motion!'

All the villagers burst into cheers of relief and Cassie even grabbed Silky in a hug. 'Wonderful!' she enthused. 'Remember, just follow The Way: all paths eventually lead to Geminopolis.'

Silky assured Cassie they'd follow the road, and the fairies made their way to the black-and-white checkered path. Pinx hung back for a moment, picking up Bizzy's coin. She turned it over in her hand and her jaw dropped.

'Bizzy!' Pinx screamed, flying to catch up with the other fairies. 'This coin has two heads! There's no way we could have won the toss!'

'Oooh,' Bizzy winced. 'That's a Big Bizzy Blunder.'

Pinx was livid, but Mel cut the tension. She tossed an arm around Pinx and laughed. 'Leave it. At least we'll get to see a new town, right?'

Pinx smiled and let Mel lead her off after the other fairies, but she couldn't shake the feeling that they had just made a terribly bad decision.

Chapter Five
The Right Path?

After several hours on foot following the black-and-white chequered tiles of The Way, the six fairies were exhausted. And when Mel got tired, she got cranky.

'How much longer until we're there?' she moaned.

'You heard the people in the last town,' Silky reminded her. '"Quite a while", they said, but, "follow The Way and you'll get there".'

'That's what *everyone* has said,' Mel grumbled. 'But we don't seem to be getting any closer at all.'

Mel wasn't wrong. Though right now they were in a fairly uninhabited forest, they had walked through countless towns, hamlets and cities, from primitive villages to bustling metropolises. Each was filled with doubles, all of whom seemed to be noticeably different, though the fairies were sure no pair was quite so dissimilar as Mel and Melody.

'It'd be faster and easier if we could fly,' Mel said, gazing pointedly at Melody.

'It *is* harder to walk,' Melody admitted, 'but think of all the people and places we'd have missed if we just flew over them. And everyone has been so excited that we're getting our Dance of the Doubles assignments!'

'Really?' Mel asked, stunned. 'You're *happy* that we're walking? Honestly, does *nothing* get you frustrated?'

Melody almost said something, but then she set her lips in a straight line and continued moving forwards. Silky bit her tongue and held down a laugh. She didn't have the heart to point out that Melody did indeed seem to get frustrated by one thing: Mel.

'Whoa!' Bizzy suddenly cried. 'Which way shall we go?'

After nothing but a single, clear path for their entire journey, the six fairies had come to a divide in The Way. Two stone arches marked the gateways to the different paths.

'Cassie told us all branches lead to Geminopolis,' Pinx remembered. 'Maybe it doesn't really matter.'

But Silky had already peered down both branches. 'I think it does matter,' she said. 'The branches are doubles. And they look like all the other doubles we've seen: completely different. They might both get us to Geminopolis, but I think the trips would be very, very different.'

The other fairies followed Silky's lead and peered down the two branches. True to form in the Land of Doubles, they looked exactly the same – and yet entirely different. Both were covered by a thick canopy of trees, both had the exact same number and placement of rocks, flowers and smaller plants; both had the same animals darting about. Yet on the right-hand path, all these things were vibrant and beautiful, while everything on the left-hand path looked withered and menacing. On the right-hand path, The Way shone brightly, as if it were tended carefully. The left-hand path was strewn with earth and barely looked used.

'What do you think, Petal?' Silky asked. 'Can the plants and animals tell you anything?'

Petal concentrated at the mouth of each pathway, then shrugged and shook her head. 'None of them are really talking,' she said. 'The right-hand path certainly *seems* friendlier though. The plants there are singing to themselves . . . they just sound happier.'

'They're singing?' Melody asked brightly, and Pinx and Mel shared an exasperated glance.

'Singing isn't enough to make it the right path,' said Pinx.

'It's not *just* the singing,' Melody countered. 'The right-hand path is nicer and prettier. It just feels like the better choice.'

'It *feels* like the better choice!' Mel scoffed. 'I'm sorry, but I'd rather not risk my life on what *feels* right. What if the right-hand side looks so lovely because it's a trap?'

'It doesn't look like a trap,' Melody said quietly.

'Of course it doesn't *look* like a trap! If it *looked* like a trap, it wouldn't *be* a trap!' Mel cried.

'Mel has a point,' Bizzy said. 'What if the path is the opposite of the way it looks?'

'Or what if we're thinking about it too hard?' Silky asked. 'Sometimes things really are what they seem, and I think the right-hand path seems safer.'

'So we're at a stalemate again,' Mel

declared, her eyes flashing impishly. 'Bet you're glad you brought me on to the team.'

'Another toss up?' Bizzy offered, and quickly magicked up a new coin, being careful to check that this one had both a head *and* a tail.

This time, Pinx chose heads. As before, Bizzy threw the coin into the air and they all watched until it landed on the ground, tail side up.

'We seriously need to come up with a better way to break ties,' Pinx complained as Silky led the group into the right-hand path. She was the last to walk through the archway and, the moment she did, a stone wall slammed down behind her, closing off the exit.

Apparently, choosing a branch of The Way was a permanent decision.

'It's so beautiful!' Melody gushed. And it was.

For several minutes, they walked through

an absolute paradise. The high canopy of leafy trees created a stunning dome of green above them, large blossoms burst into vibrant bloom as the fairies walked past, a herd of deer pranced along beside them.

But all too soon, the landscape changed. The trees that arced over the path grew shorter and shorter as the fairies moved forwards, until what had been a high canopy of leaves became the ceiling of a tunnel so low and cramped that the fairies could no longer stand upright and walk beneath it. They crawled. The Way had changed as well: it was now dirty, chipped and bramble-covered. Even the wildlife had changed. The deer were gone, replaced by the screeching of fearsome, unseen creatures.

'Is it just me,' Bizzy asked, 'or is this a Particularly Petrifying Path?

'It could be worse,' Silky murmured. 'It could be raining.'

That's when it started to rain: a thunderstorm that drenched the fairies to the skin.

Pinx grimaced and looked up to the sky. 'That wasn't a request!'

With nothing for it but to continue, the fairies kept crawling along the wet and increasingly mucky Way, until finally the downpour ended. At the same time, the canopy of trees opened up once again to reveal a beautiful clearing, dotted with charming, two-storey wooden houses, each with its own lovely flower garden.

'What a sweet little village,' Melody sighed.

'And those flowers,' Petal agreed. 'I've never seen roses so large.' She stepped forwards eagerly for a closer look – and triggered an alarm that blared across the landscape.

Immediately, a sea of people poured out of the charming houses, all wielding clubs and sticks that they pointed at the fairies. At the same time, several other people – guards, it seemed – leaped down from the trees and grabbed Petal. It all happened so quickly that the fairies didn't have time to do anything more than scream in shock.

'We don't like intruders here!' the guard sneered to the fairies as he held Petal in his grip. 'If you value your friend, you'll do as we say.'

Silky, Pinx, Petal, Melody and Mel exchanged nervous glances as they quickly considered their options. They were hugely outnumbered and the guards held Petal tightly. If they tried to fight back, could they succeed without risking Petal's life? The odds were not in their favour.

'Please don't hurt her,' Silky begged the guards. 'We'll do what you ask.'

'Perfect. Walk this way, please.' The guard sounded polite, but his smile was far from friendly. Still gripping Petal, and backed up by all the armed townsfolk, the guards led the fairies forwards. As they walked, Silky looked meaningfully to Petal — what about the plants and animals? Could they help? Petal knew what Silky was wondering and shook her head. The plants and animals here were not the type to listen to Petal. She was completely helpless.

'Halt!' cried the guards, and the fairies saw

why they had been taken to this spot. In front of them sat a huge pool of what looked like soft mud. Then the guard holding Petal tossed a rock on to it, which was quickly sucked down into nothingness.

'Quicksand,' said the guard, grinning. 'Step in.'

'Don't do it!' Petal cried, her eyes growing wide. And while Silky agreed that stepping into a pool of quicksand wouldn't be their best plan, she didn't know what else to do. With so many townsfolk ready to attack, could the fairies really fight back and escape? Could all of them possibly survive? Could any of them?

Melody gulped and looked sheepishly at Pinx and Mel. 'This path might have been a trap,' she admitted.

Chapter Six
Another Way

The guard holding Petal was running out of patience. 'Into the quicksand ... *now*,' he commanded, tightening his grip on her until she cried out. Then suddenly ...

'ROOOOAAAARRRRR!'

Out of nowhere, a massive beast lurched towards the guards. It towered three times their size and was covered head to toe with orange, razor-sharp porcupine spikes. Its red eyes glowed with ferocity and, as it rose up on its hind legs, it opened its mouth to reveal rows of shark-like fangs. It growled again, a sound so fierce that every creature within earshot cowered in fear. Even the fairies grabbed for one another and held each other close.

For a single second, the guards and the townsfolk froze, too terrified to move. They considered the clubs and sticks in their hands. They considered the hideous titan of a beast before them.

Then the creature blew a plume of searing hot fire that blasted into the air above all their heads.

The guards and townsfolk screamed for dear life and scattered. They raced into their homes, locking and blockading the doors.

That left the fairies alone with the monster. It turned to them . . . and winked!

'*No way*,' Silky said as realisation dawned.

'Is this Magnificently Malevolent Monster . . . *MEL?*' Bizzy asked.

The hideous beast grinned and with a wickedly delighted laugh, it turned itself back into Melody's double. 'In the flesh!' she lilted. 'Or, you know, the spikes.'

'You're AWESOME!' Pinx cried, wrapping

Mel in a huge hug.

'Yeah, well, you know . . .' Mel began with false modesty.

'I don't think I've ever met an animal I loved more than you,' Petal enthused. 'But we should get out of here before the townsfolk get over their fright.'

'Oh, I don't think that'll be happening for a *looong* time,' Pinx laughed, but the fairies still walked back to The Way and followed it out of the tree canopy where it rejoined with the other branch – the one they *hadn't* taken.

As they walked, Melody shook her head, confused. 'I don't understand,' she said to Mel, 'I can only transform into things I know really well. Isn't it the same for you?'

'Yes,' Mel said.

'OK, but . . . I don't know anything *like* that terrible beast! How would you?' Melody asked.

Mel laughed. 'It's how I imagine myself when I get really, really angry – *that's* how I know it so well!'

'That's brilliant,' Silky said, laughing. 'It's a

lot like how I imagine Pinx when she gets cross.'

Pinx opened her mouth, mock-insulted, then shot back, 'Really? Because it looked to me more like the inner Silky during a flash attack! ROOOOAAAARRRRR!' She bared her teeth and made her hands into claws and all three of the fairies laughed.

Behind them, Melody walked with Petal and Bizzy, shaking her head as she looked at Mel. 'It's just so strange,' she told her friends. 'I know a lot of the doubles have their differences, but shouldn't Mel and I have *something* in common?'

'I'm sure there is something,' Petal said, but she hoped Melody wouldn't ask her to suggest what it could be.

'Maybe the Gemini Locket makes mistakes, like I do,' Bizzy suggested. 'Mel could be its version of a Basic Bizzy Blunder.'

Melody was still thinking about this

possibility when the fairies came to another divide in The Way, each path again marked off by a large stone archway. Unlike the last fork, this one led to two very different routes: one curved down a rolling path to sand dunes and a beach; the other up towards farmland.

'Weird,' Bizzy noted. 'The paths are Definitely Decidedly Different. Shouldn't they be doubles?'

'Maybe each path has its own set of doubles,' Silky suggested.

Petal couldn't take her eyes off the farmland. 'It looks a bit like Fairyland Farms, doesn't it?' she sighed. 'I can just picture Uncle Delta there.'

'I like it too,' Melody said dreamily. 'Listen – you can hear the songbirds.'

'You like that path?' Mel asked. 'Then I choose the other one.'

Melody gasped. 'That's just mean!'

'It's not. It's common sense,' Mel retorted.

'Look at your choices: you wanted to talk to the dancing villagers – that started the whole mess. You wanted to follow The Way – that took us here to the middle of nowhere. You wanted to take the pretty path in the road – we almost got swallowed by quicksand! Seems to me the only sensible thing to do is listen closely to you, then do the exact opposite of what you suggest!'

'Nothing personal, Melody, but she does have an excellent point,' Pinx said.

'She does not!' Melody shot back, then turned to Silky and Bizzy. 'Does she?'

'Not *exactly* . . .' Bizzy hedged, and Melody's insulted eyes grew wide.

'No, she does *not* have a point,' Silky said firmly. 'I agreed with you on all those choices, and I agree that we should take the path to the farmland.'

'That's three against three again,' Mel said, rolling her eyes.

Bizzy opened her mouth to speak, but Pinx cut her off. 'No way – I am *not* flipping another coin.'

'What if we split up?' Mel offered. Everyone gasped, and even Pinx looked at her in disbelief. 'What?' Mel protested.

'We *never* split up,' Melody said. 'Not unless we're forced to.'

'Well, why not?' Mel asked. 'If three of us want to go one way, and three of us want to go the other, why not just do it?'

'Because we could run into Talon,' Silky said, 'and we're more likely to get his Talisman half if we're all together.'

'So, it would only work if we had a way to keep track of one another, no matter where we are,' concluded Pinx.

'Oh!' Bizzy cried excitedly, then raised her arms in the air, waved her wand as she recited a spell, and POOF! Two small cages appeared on the ground, each containing an adorable small yellow bird with a peach-coloured face. Though the birds were in separate cages, they cuddled as close to one another as possible, leaning their beaks out between the bars to touch.

'Aaah!' Melody cooed. 'They're so cute! Are they lovebirds?'

'They're Truelovebirds,' Bizzy said proudly. 'Truelovebirds are so Lost in Lifelong Love that they will always find one another, no matter what. If we split up, and one of our groups needs the other one for any reason, they can just release their Truelovebird and follow it to the other group!'

They all agreed it was a perfect solution, so the six fairies said their goodbyes for the moment. Each group picked up a Truelovebird then Pinx, Mel and Bizzy took the path down to the beach while Melody, Silky and Petal took the path to the farms.

As they walked through the stone archways that defined their branches of The Way, rock walls again slammed down behind them.

'We absolutely chose the right path,' Petal declared several minutes later, and Silky and Melody had to agree.

No matter how lovely the beach path might be, the farm path was superior. Its meadows were dotted with round fuzzy sheep, stout pink pigs and chubby, black-and-white dappled cows, all of them in doubled pairs, and all eager to show off their moves for the evening's Dance of the Doubles. The animals trotted gaily to The Way at the sight of the fairies and danced and twirled for their audience's approval, which the fairies gave happily. After each round of dancing, the animals pushed in close, rubbing up against Melody, Petal and Silky for hugs, petting and scratching.

It simply couldn't have been more perfect, until the animals' playful romp was interrupted by a hideously bloodcurdling and gut-wrenchingly familiar scream.

Talon was coming.

Chapter Seven
Tallie

At least, this Troll *looked* like Talon. And he was flying on an enchanted stick – sort of. Actually, he was more dangling *from* the stick, clinging to it for dear life as he kicked and flailed his legs wildly. And the more Silky, Petal and Melody listened to this Troll's scream, the more they realised it was more of a panicked wail than a threat.

'Oh-help-me-I'm-going-to-fall-oh-no-oh-no-oh-noooo!' he shouted.

The fairies were fascinated by this and couldn't take their eyes off him as his stick lost all control and fell closer . . . closer . . .

'Duck!' Silky finally screamed, and the three of them leaped out of the way as he crashed into the meadow, frightening the sheep, pigs and cows, who scattered everywhere.

Silky, Petal and Melody were about to release their Truelovebird so their friends could help them fight when they were stopped in their tracks by a sound they had never heard before.

This Troll was crying.

'Please come back!' he called out to the animals, tears streaming down his face. 'I'm so sorry I scared you. It was the stick! I'd never enchanted anything before and it took off so quickly and I'm *so* afraid of heights. Can you forgive me?'

As he spoke, the farm animals looked at each other quizzically, unsure what to make of the weeping Troll. Deciding he was harmless enough, they trotted over to him. The minute one of the sheep was close enough, the grateful Troll threw himself on the creature for a giant, weepy hug – then started sneezing wildly.

'Oh, please don't be insulted,' he gently pleaded with the animal between sniffs and sobs. 'It's just my allergies. And here I am without a handkerchief, which is so silly because I'm allergic to so many things and, of course, the littlest things always make me cry.'

Silky, Petal and Melody had been watching all this time, agape. Silky, however, had an idea of what was really going on and tentatively stepped forwards to get the Troll's attention.

'Um . . . Talon?'

He screamed in horror and leaped behind the flock of sheep for cover. 'Talon!' he cried. 'Where? Are you with him?'

Silky smiled, completely understanding now. 'No,' she said, 'but you're Talon's double, aren't you.'

'Yes,' the other Talon admitted unhappily, 'but please don't compare me to that awful creature. He's so mean!' Then he gasped and his eyes grew wide with recognition. 'But you know that! You must be the Faraway Fairies! Oh, the things Talon said about you. He's so horrible, I couldn't bear to be near him a second longer.' He looked around him, taking in his broken stick and untidy robes. 'Not that I do so very well on my own ...'

'But you don't have to be on your own,' Melody jumped in. 'You can stay with us.' She turned to Silky and Petal. 'He can, can't he? I mean, I know he's Talon, but at the same time ... he's not.'

'Not at all!' the double declared. 'Please, don't even call me his name!'

'What should we call you then?' Petal asked.

Talon's double thought it over, then smiled. 'Tallie,' he said. 'Much more friendly, don't you think? Now if only I could *look* different from that monstrous Troll, I'd feel much happier.'

Petal grinned. 'I have an idea.' She bent down to pluck a leaf . . .

'You're not going to hurt that plant, are you?' Tallie worried.

Petal's smile spread even wider: Tallie had just endeared himself to Petal for life. She assured him that the plants were offering up their leaves willingly then finished picking a selection – choosing carefully so as not to set off the Troll's allergies – which she wove into a garland for his head.

'I love it,' Tallie enthused after Melody transformed into a mirror so he could catch his reflection. 'I'll never take it off!'

Silky looked up at the sky. Judging by the suns, it was already late afternoon, which meant there was a decent chance they'd still be in the Land by sundown. 'We should probably get on to Geminopolis,' Silky said, then turned to Tallie. 'You are joining us, aren't you?'

The Troll smiled warmly. 'I would be more than honoured to join you,' he said happily.

As the foursome continued along The Way, the fairies were amazed by how perfectly Tallie fitted into their group. He was really lovely: so clumsy and uncertain, and yet so sensitive, caring and sweet. Quite the polar opposite of Talon.

Tallie confirmed what the fairies already suspected. Talon had tried to enchant himself back home to drop off his half of the Gemini

Locket, but he'd failed because Tallie tied Talon to the Land. No matter how many times Talon tried to zap himself away, he only bounced to a different spot in the Land of Doubles. It made him furious, not to mention even more eager to find the other half of the Gemini Locket.

Tallie knew Talon would find the fairies before long; he had seen Talon consulting his crystal, which apparently helped guide him on the fairies' path.

The fairies hadn't known this before, but it wasn't surprising. It explained why Talon always seemed to know just where they were, no matter how large the Land.

At long last, The Way led the group to Geminopolis, which felt like something out of a storybook. Twin horses pulled twin carriages down twin elm-tree-lined streets, twin buildings sported twin turrets and domes and, of course, the town teemed with doubles, all

getting ready for the Dance of the Doubles. As the only non-doubles around, Silky, Petal, Melody and Tallie got a great deal of attention, so it wasn't hard to ask directions to the office of the Ministers of Motion.

As singletons, the group was led right in, and the Ministers leaped from their twin desks at the sight of them. Like all the doubles, the Ministers looked exactly alike – except not quite. While both had long handlebar moustaches, one Minister's curved up in what looked like a giant smile, while the other Minister's drooped down like a sad mouth.

At the exact same time, they each took ten steps towards Tallie and the fairies, put their hands on their hips and leaned in towards the group to ask in unison, 'Who are you, and where are your doubles?' The only difference was that the smiley-moustached Minister said it sweetly, while the droopy-moustached Minister said it with a growl.

Silky explained the situation: that she and Petal had no doubles, but Melody and Tallie did. They simply weren't together.

'But if they're not together, how can they do the Dance of the Doubles?' one Minister asked as the other roared the question.

Melody stepped forwards. 'If we're here at sunset, I'm happy to do the Dance with my Double, sirs. Please teach me the steps and I'll share them with her.'

The Ministers turned to Tallie and one asked sweetly while the other bellowed, 'But what about him?'

'Me!' Tallie squeaked. 'Dance with *Talon*? Oh, no. No, no, no. That would be impossible. Absolutely impossible.' He turned to the fairies and wrinkled his nose. 'Can you even imagine?'

Silky, Petal and Melody had to giggle at the thought. Talon dancing at all was ridiculous, but dancing a duet with Tallie?

There was no way in the universe that would happen!

The smiley-moustached Minister grew pale while the droopy-moustached Minister became red. 'You don't understand,' they said. 'The Land of Doubles needs the energy of *every* double, no matter how newly created. If this troll and his double are here in the Land and don't do the Dance, our world will not survive.'

Chapter Eight
The Inner Talon

With sunset looming closer, and the importance of the Dance of the Doubles so real, it was clear that both Melody *and* Tallie should get assigned and learn Dance parts – even though the idea of getting Talon to dance with Tallie still seemed impossible. Melody, of course, learned her steps immediately, right there in the Ministers of Motion's office, and did them with such grace that even the droopy-moustached Minister was enchanted. Tallie's dancing was not so brilliant, but Melody assured both him and the Ministers that she'd help him get it right by sunset.

Now the fairies were ready to meet up with Mel, Pinx and Bizzy again. Since neither

Melody nor Tallie could fly on their own, Tallie enchanted an elegant hat stand belonging to the happier of the two Ministers. This would be their ride, and the two climbed on in preparation for take-off. Of course, since Tallie had some problems with his balance, Silky and Petal planned to hold on to the hat stand and help steer. With all that arranged, Petal opened the door of the Truelovebird's cage and . . .

. . . the bird zipped out the window and flew completely out of sight in less than a second!

The fairies' jaws dropped.

'Where did he go?' Melody asked.

'He *really* wanted to see his true love,'

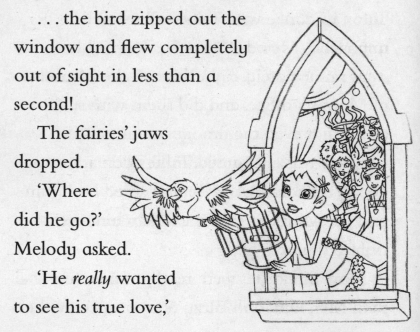

Petal said, amazed, 'so he flew as quickly as he could.'

'Now what do we do?' Silky asked. 'That bird was our only way to find Mel, Pinx and Bizzy! Without it we can't get together for the Dance.'

'Nonsense,' said the Ministers of Motion, the droopy-moustached one in a huff and the other with a chuckle. They turned to Melody and continued, 'If you have a double, she's part of you. You don't need a bird to find her; you can *feel* where she is!'

Melody looked dubious. 'You don't know my double,' she said softly. 'I can't think of anyone who's *less* a part of me than Mel.'

'Just try,' urged the Ministers, one more gently than the other.

Melody still looked doubtful, but she closed her eyes, took a deep breath . . .

'Wait!' Silky jumped in. 'If you can feel Mel then Tallie can feel Talon. Why don't we go to him first and get the other half of the Gemini Locket before sunset. Then we can leave and we won't have to worry about Talon doing the Dance.' Silky turned to Tallie, who already looked uncomfortable. She took his hand and asked, 'Tallie? Will you do it?'

'I don't want to,' said Tallie, scrunching up his face in disgust at the very idea of connecting with Talon. Then he took a deep breath and met Silky's eyes. 'But I'll do it for the three of you.'

'Thank you, Tallie,' Silky said, and both Petal and Melody smiled their thanks as well.

'What do I have to do?' Tallie asked the Ministers of Motion. One rolled his eyes while the other smiled indulgently.

'Just concentrate,' they said in unison. '*Feel* your double.'

Reluctantly, Tallie closed his eyes and concentrated. The fairies watched him.

Nothing.

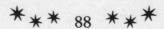

'Keep trying, Tallie,' Silky urged gently.

Tallie relaxed deeper into his thoughts, really trying to feel some kind of twinship with Talon. Suddenly, his face contorted like he might be ill.

'I know that expression!' Silky cried. 'You've found him!'

'Yes,' Tallie grimaced, his eyes still closed, 'I can feel him. It's like . . . sweaty socks in my mouth. Disgusting!' His eyes snapped open. 'But it's what we want. I can get us to him. Hold on, Melody – we're off to find Talon!'

Melody wrapped her arms around Tallie's waist and he kicked the enchanted hat stand into action, rocketing it out of the window.

'AAAAAAHHH!' they screamed as it spiralled wildly out of control.

Silky and Petal shared a quick look of alarm then raced out of the window after the pair. They grabbed the hat stand and steadied it before it could plummet to the ground.

'Thanks,' Tallie smiled sheepishly. 'I guess I got a little overexcited. Are you OK, Melody?'

'Of course,' Melody said kindly, though there was still fear in her eyes.

'Great!' Silky said, grinning. 'Then let's go and find Talon!'

Tallie pointed in the direction of his double and the foursome sped off to challenge their greatest enemy.

Chapter Nine
Double Trouble

Voilà!' cried Mel, spinning round so Pinx could see. After busily beachcombing, she had decorated her outfit with a stunning array of shells and bits of broken coral. She looked dazzling.

'I *love* it!' Pinx shouted. She had already plucked up any pink bits of shell she could find and woven them into her lightning-bolt pigtails. Her eyes dancing, she turned to Bizzy. 'Your turn – ready for a Pinx and Mel makeover?'

Bizzy gave an uncomfortable half smile. 'That would be fun . . . but shouldn't we be doing something else?'

It was awkward for Bizzy to have to say this. After all, she'd been the one to start the fun. The minute they'd taken the path, her eyes had grown wide with delight. 'Look at those sand dunes!' she'd squealed, marvelling at the giant double mounds that peppered the beach. 'What do you think? Should we roll 'down?'

'YES!' screamed Pinx and Mel, and the three climbed up to the highest dune then rolled all the way down, howling with laughter as they bounced along. As they dizzily brushed themselves off, Mel suggested the ride would be even better with a sledge.

Thrilled with the idea, Bizzy tried to magic one up, but a bed appeared instead — which turned out to be perfect! All three fairies climbed aboard the mattress and slid down together, shrieking as the wind whipped through their hair.

After several more runs, the beautiful double seashells that had washed up along the water's edge had captivated Pinx and Mel.

Bizzy had to admit the final results were astounding, but it didn't change the fact that they were here in the Land on a mission, and she was starting to feel guilty about simply playing around.

'I just wonder if we shouldn't be Troll-Tracking Talon,' Bizzy offered gently, not wanting to get Pinx and Mel annoyed.

They shrugged off Bizzy's concerns. 'Looking for Talon is a waste. He could be anywhere,' Mel said.

'Silky said the same thing,' Pinx reminded Bizzy. 'If Talon wants the Locket, he'll find *us*.'

'At which point we'll trounce him, get his half of the Locket and follow our Truelovebird to the others!' Mel added.

'Or *they'll* find Talon and they'll send their Truelovebird to us,' Pinx concluded. 'Now, come here. Those curls are dying for some Pinx and Mel magic.'

'OK . . .' Bizzy agreed tentatively, settling

herself between Pinx and Mel so they could work on her, 'but shouldn't we at least head to Geminopolis to learn the Dance of the Doubles?'

Mel scoffed. 'As if me dancing with Melody is going to make a difference. Every double here is going to dance. Believe me, we won't be missed.' That did *seem* logical. And it was awfully fun to have Pinx and Mel doing her hair.

When they finally turned her towards the ocean, Bizzy's smile practically lit up the horizon. 'I'm Simply Strikingly Stunning!' she raved. As if to emphasise her joy, an angelic voice rang out in her head, singing a gorgeously triumphant tune.

Mel and Pinx scrunched up their eyebrows and turned towards the sand dunes, and Bizzy realised the song wasn't coming from inside her head at all.

'Who's singing?' Pinx asked.

'I don't know, but the music is almost as magnificent as Melody's!' Bizzy noticed Mel's glare, then quickly added, 'And Mel's, I'm sure. Let's go and see who it is!'

'Because the song's beautiful?' Pinx asked, laughing. 'Who are you, Melody?' But even as she chided Bizzy, the two started towards the dunes, following the music.

'No!' Mel stopped them, her eyes narrowing as she thought it through. 'This could be a trap. Think about it: Talon fought *Melody* for the Locket. He would think she has our half. He might even think I'm her, though how anyone in their right mind would make that mistake is beyond me. But if Talon did want to trick Melody and lure her away, wouldn't he try to do it with beautiful music?'

Neither Pinx nor Bizzy had thought of it that way, but Mel was absolutely right. So instead of heading straight for the sound of the song, Pinx, Mel and Bizzy set down their Truelovebird and walked the long way around, careful to keep themselves hidden behind sand dunes. Then they peeked out and saw Talon.

The hideous Troll was crouching between two dunes. He grinned with wicked glee, holding up a small music box and licking his lips in anticipation.

Then Pinx smiled. She had a plan and she whispered it quickly to Mel and Bizzy who nodded in agreement.

'TWEEET!'

Suddenly, the Truelovebird that had raced away from Silky, Melody and Petal zipped overhead on its way to meet its mate. Its call made Talon look up – and right into the eyes of Bizzy. She stood alone, holding something very familiar to Talon: the other half of the Gemini Locket.

'Are you Looking for this Lovely Little

Locket?' she asked.

Talon sneered, baring his yellow teeth. 'Not any more,' he growled. 'Now I've found it – and I'm going to make it mine. *All* mine!'

He lunged for the Locket, but Bizzy pointed her wand to the beach under Talon's feet. 'Slippy, slippo, sploosh!'

Instantly, the sand mushed into mud and Talon's feet slipped out from under him, sending him sprawling into the mire. Bizzy giggled happily, but Talon was far from defeated.

He quickly rose and picked up handful after handful of the dirt, hurling mud balls at Bizzy while reciting spells that she knew would turn the harmless muck into a trap. Bizzy darted and dodged to avoid the missiles, flying so quickly she couldn't catch her breath long enough to recite a counter-spell.

Talon had Bizzy cornered; he knew it was only a matter of time before one of his

missiles hit its mark.

'Where are your friends, little fairy?' he
hissed as he threw. 'I saw three of you on the
beach. Were they supposed to come and
ambush me while you had my attention?
Looks like they've let you down.'

Talon laughed, hurling the mud even faster,
but he had no idea how close he was to the
truth. Bizzy *was* distracting him, but she
wasn't alone. The Locket she held was not

the real Locket at all, but Mel transformed to look just like it. While Bizzy and Mel had Talon's attention, an invisible Pinx was searching Talon's cloak for his half of the Locket. The cloak was so large and billowy that Talon didn't even notice her. There was only one small hitch: Pinx hadn't realised how horrible Talon's festering body would smell. The stench was like poison in her lungs and it burned her eyes and nose. The only way she could function was to hold her breath.

Finally Pinx saw it: the other half of the Gemini Locket tucked into a pocket towards the back of the cloak. Unfortunately, she was running out of air. She *had* to take a breath – but a breath of Talon's noxious odour would certainly make Pinx pass out. She darted far away from Talon's cloak and took a huge lungful of air just as Bizzy finally cried out, 'Freezo Frozo Fricklefrost!'

The mud that surrounded Talon immediately turned to solid ice, causing him to slip and slide and fall flat on his back.

Pinx almost laughed out loud, but she didn't want Talon to notice her. Instead, she became visible for just a moment – far behind Talon's back – and signalled to Bizzy that she almost had the Locket. Bizzy only needed to distract Talon for another moment . . .

'Leave them alone, Talon, and give us the Locket!' Silky screamed as she and Petal soared into view, pulling Tallie and Melody on their enchanted hat stand.

Talon, Bizzy, and Pinx all looked up, surprised.

'You!' Talon cried, his face twisting at the sight of Tallie. 'You pathetic excuse for a Troll! I told you I never wanted to see you again!'

As Talon raged, Petal and Silky seized their chance to turn their powers on him.

Silky shot white-hot bolts of light at the Troll, while Petal rallied several pairs of doubled crabs and lobsters to race out of the ocean and attack him with their pincers. Talon screamed as they nipped his skin and one of the light bolts hit him in the foot. Then, with a shriek, Tallie tried to deliver the final blow. He leaped off the hat stand to tackle Talon, but the Troll had realised it was time to retreat.

Talon blurted a quick spell in Trollish, and his crystal flashed him away from all the attacks, leaving Tallie to slam face-first into the sand.

As Silky and Petal guided Melody and the hat stand gently on to the sand next to Tallie, Mel turned back into herself and stalked towards them.

'What were you thinking?' she shouted. 'Now you've gone and ruined everything!'

Chapter Ten
The Last Straw

Tallie was weeping.

For Bizzy and Pinx, this was the most bizarre sight in the world. They knew he was not the same Troll as their enemy, but he still *looked* just like Talon, and a sobbing, despondent Talon seemed impossible.

Mel, of course, was nowhere near as thrown by the appearance of another double, so it didn't stop her from railing at Tallie and the fairies one bit. She told them all about the plan they had ruined and just how close Pinx had been to grabbing the other half of the Gemini Locket.

Tallie felt guilty. 'It's true!' he wailed. 'We're awful! We're horrible! We've ruined everything! Ohhh, I'm so ashamed!' He burst into a fresh round of sobs, curling into a small ball in the sand.

Bizzy felt bad for him. 'Mel's not saying that you meant to mess things up,' she reassured him.

'It was just a mistake . . . a mishap . . . a —'

'Monstrosity!' Tallie bawled. Melody placed a hand on his back and began to hum softly in the hope of calming him down. It worked enough that he could finally speak without interrupting himself with choking sobs. 'Now it's almost sunset, and if Melody and Mel and

Talon and I don't do the Dance of the Doubles together this Land won't survive!'

'I think that's a bit of an exaggeration,' Pinx said.

'No, it isn't,' Silky said. 'The Ministers of Motion told us all the doubles must dance for the Land to survive. Even new doubles.'

'Can we find Talon, get his half of the Locket and get back down the Ladder before sunset?' Melody asked.

The fairies studied the sky. The twin suns sat low on the horizon. They had perhaps an hour or so before sunset. It wasn't likely they'd make it in time.

'Maybe we could just take *our* half of the Locket back to the Tree,' Bizzy suggested

'But half a Talisman won't keep the Land of Doubles tied to the Tree. It would never come back to the top of the Ladder,' Pinx said.

'And half a Talisman won't help the Tree get better,' Petal added.

'But it *will* keep the Land of Doubles out of Talon's control,' Bizzy said. 'And if we all go, Mel and Tallie won't be here, so it won't matter that they don't do the Dance of the Doubles.'

'That makes sense,' Silky said, 'except . . .' She looked meaningfully at Mel and Tallie and Bizzy remembered what Witch Whisper had told them.

'Ohhh,' she nodded in understanding.

'What? What is it? What are you talking about?' Tallie asked. He had noticed the uncomfortable glances between the fairies and looked worried. Melody tried to explain it gently.

'Doubles are tied to this Land,' she said, 'which means you and Mel can't come with us to the Tree. You can't leave.'

'You mean *we* can't leave,' Mel said pointedly to Melody. 'You're a double too.'

Obvious as this was, Melody hadn't

thought of it that way before. She felt she was the original and only Mel was the double. But Mel was right. Just as Talon couldn't leave once Tallie arrived, Melody wouldn't be able to leave either.

'But this is terrible,' Melody said, too shocked to lift her voice above a whisper.

'It's just as bad for me, you know. Do you think I want to be stuck with *you* forever?' Mel exploded.

Melody looked at Mel, surprised. 'What? That wasn't what I meant! I just –'

'You make me so angry!' Mel cried, unable to contain her frustration. 'Just because we *look* the same, you expect me to be *exactly* like you, and you get all sulky when I'm not! Meanwhile, *you're* a disaster! You don't think anything through, you've got this ridiculous idea that everything pretty in the universe is just delightful and you've turned what was supposed to be a brilliant adventure into a terrible mess! But you know what the most infuriating thing is? You don't even realise it! You *never* get upset! You just go along botching everything up for the rest of us and smiling about it!'

Melody felt like she'd been kicked in the stomach. No one had ever spoken to her like this. She couldn't even meet Mel's eyes. 'I understand that you're upset, but shouting about it won't solve anything,' she objected quietly.

'Yes, it *will*!' Mel shouted. 'I'm furious, and if I want to shout about it, I will! And another thing . . .'

But Melody was no longer there. She couldn't bear Mel's anger and had turned into a beautiful hummingbird that flitted through the air, humming a soothing tune.

'Oh, no,' Mel said, 'you're not getting away *that* easily!'

In the blink of an eye, Mel turned into a

huge Venus Flytrap that stretched out its mouth and snapped wildly at the hummingbird. To escape, Melody became a pretty stone fountain, bubbling happily and peacefully. To retaliate, Mel turned herself from a Venus Flytrap to an angry piranha, thrashing in the fountain and making waves in its water.

Throughout all this, Tallie and the fairies could only look on, stunned and helpless.

Finally, Melody turned back to herself and Mel immediately did the same. But Melody didn't look like herself at all. Her cheeks were flushed pink with anger and she even raised her voice as she leaned in close to her double.

'You really think I'm any happier with you than you are with me?' she asked. 'I thought it would be wonderful to have a double, but it's not, it's horrible! You're selfish, you're rude ... there's *nothing* in you that I respect and yet you're *connected* to me! Do you have any idea how awful that makes me feel?'

'Yes, I do!' Mel retorted. 'I know *exactly* how awful it is! I don't want anything to do with you, either. *Nothing!*'

'Good!' Melody continued. 'Because if I thought there was even the littlest part of myself in you, I'd ... I'd ... I don't know *what* I'd do!'

Mel was about to scream her response, but stopped.

Something Melody had said clicked with her and she leaned back. The beginnings of a smile began to form on her face. 'Really?' she finally said to Melody. 'You don't know *what* you'd do? Because if I thought there was even the littlest bit of you in me, I know *exactly* what I'd do.'

Melody looked shocked for a moment. Was Mel threatening her? Then she understood. The pink flush of anger faded from her cheeks and she smiled. 'Do you think it would work?'

Mel looked back at the suns, dropping ever lower in the sky. 'It'll be close,' she said, 'but I think we have just enough time to try.'

In perfect tandem, Mel and Melody ran to Tallie. Each of them took one of his arms as they helped him to his feet.

'I know you hate to do it, but we want you to lead us to Talon,' Melody said gently.

'Not quite yet, though,' Mel added. 'First we want to get to know one another properly.'

And as the Twinkletune doubles led Tallie away to chat – stopping to release the remaining Truelovebird, so the pair could happily fly away together – Petal, Pinx and Bizzy could only watch, dumbfounded.

'Does anyone know what just happened?' Pinx asked. 'Because I haven't got a clue.'

'I think I do,' said Silky, smiling. 'I just hope it works.'

Chapter Eleven
The Dance of the Doubles

Silky, Petal, Bizzy and Pinx held tightly to the flying hat stand on which Tallie, Mel and Melody sat. With only a few minutes before sunset, the group raced across the sky, letting Tallie point the way towards Talon.

'There he is!' Tallie cried, but only loud enough for the fairies to hear. They didn't want to get Talon's attention. Not yet.

Below them sprawled the fairy tale town of Geminopolis. As before, doubles filled the streets, but now they weren't practising for the Dance of the Doubles. Instead they stared in shock at Talon the Troll, who held a prize in his fist: two hamster-sized Ministers of Motion.

'Hostages,' Silky realised. 'He knows we'll come for the Locket and he thinks we'll trade our half for the ministers.'

Moving quickly, the fairies eased the hat stand to the ground behind a building, then Silky, Petal, Bizzy and Pinx flew out to face the wicked Troll.

'Let them go and give us the Locket, Talon!' Silky cried.

'That's funny,' Talon laughed. 'You say that like you have the upper hand. But if you don't give *me* the Locket, I'll crush these two doubles into nothing!' Suddenly, the Ministers both bit down on Talon's hand.

'Ow!' he cried. 'Bad little doubles,' he scolded. 'Now look what I have to do.' He recited another spell in Trollish and the Ministers' mouths were sealed shut. Then he turned back to the fairies. 'Now . . . the Locket.'

'No!' cried a voice. It was Tallie, who pushed his way through the crowd to stand in front of Talon, his hands on his hips.

Talon simply scoffed. 'You!' he mocked.

'You're no threat to me! You're spineless!'

'Spineless?' echoed another voice. 'But Talon, I'm you.'

Talon's eyes grew wide as a second Tallie pushed through the crowd to stand next to the first. Yet even though the sight of this second Tallie was jarring, what really threw him were the words spoken by this Tallie. They were unthinkable.

'Me? You think you're *me*?' Talon spluttered. 'Hah! You're *nothing* like me!'

'I am,' came another voice, and a third Tallie joined the other two. 'And you're just like me,' this third Tallie continued. 'Deep inside you have to be. I wouldn't exist if I weren't part of you. You're just as sweet, as kind, as caring –'

'No!' Talon objected. 'I'm *not*!'

'Of course you are,' said the first Tallie. 'Maybe you've forgotten, but part of you is gentle and loving and cares about his fellow creatures so much it breaks your heart to even think of hurting them.'

'You're wrong!' Talon sneered, losing control. 'You know *nothing* about me! Nothing!'

'Oh, but we do,' the second Tallie said gently. 'And we know part of you wants to change. It's not too late, you know. Put down the Ministers and give us the Locket. Be who you really are.'

'Join us, Talon,' urged the third Tallie. 'Follow what's really in your heart.'

'You want to know what's really in my heart?' Talon exploded. He hurled the tiny Ministers to the ground – Bizzy quickly magicked up a fluffy pillow to catch their fall – and grabbed the three Tallies. He screamed out a spell in Trollish and his crystal flashed.

The Tallie in the middle immediately transformed into a mirror, bouncing Talon's own spell back at him. It was so powerful that

Talon was thrown back several feet and landed on the ground, unconscious.

Instantly, Talon's spells were broken as the Ministers of Motion returned to their normal size and could once again open their mouths.

Mel and Melody, who, of course, had been the other two Tallies, quickly turned back to themselves. They, Tallie and the other fairies raced over to the fallen Talon.

Pinx reached into his cloak and grabbed the other half of the Gemini Locket from its hiding place. She handed it to Silky, who produced the other Locket half and snapped them back together.

Talon was still completely motionless.

'Is he . . . dead?' Bizzy finally asked.

'No,' Petal said, sensing life still in the Troll, 'but he's badly hurt. It must have been a very strong spell.'

'Of course it was,' Mel said with a knowing look to Melody, 'he was really, really angry.'

Melody nodded. 'It's hard when you see the other side of yourself.'

'*Really* hard,' Mel admitted. She smiled at her double. 'But it's good . . . I guess.'

Melody returned the smile. 'I think it's *very* good.'

They started to come together for a hug, when . . .

'It's sunset!' the Ministers of Motion cried anxiously, waving their hands in the air in terror. 'It's time for the Dance of the Doubles!'

It was true. The Ministers of Motion were dancing as they shouted to the fairies. All of the doubles in Geminopolis were dancing in perfect unison; all except for Melody and Mel, and Tallie and Talon.

Twin lightning bolts split the sky and the ground rumbled with an earthquake that left twin cracks in the cobblestoned courtyard below their feet.

'It's really happening!' Pinx cried in dismay.

'The Land is falling apart because the doubles aren't dancing.'

'Let's do this,' Melody said to Mel, but Mel shook her head.

'I don't know the steps!' Mel objected.

'You don't need to,' Melody said, locking eyes with her double. 'You're like me, remember? I know you can do this. Will you follow my lead?'

Mel nodded, smiling at Melody. 'I'd be proud to.'

But even as the Twinkletunes began to dance in gorgeous unison, thunder cracked and twin lightning bolts struck twin elm trees, setting them on fire.

Bizzy quickly magicked up a raincloud that doused them, but she knew she couldn't keep up if the lightning kept on striking.

'The storm's not stopping!' Pinx cried.

'It's not just the storm,' Petal warned. 'All the plants are wilting. I can feel it.'

'The Land is Losing its Life!' Bizzy wailed.

'It's Tallie and Talon,' Silky said. 'They're not dancing together.'

But there was no remedy for that because Talon was still out cold.

'There's nothing we can do,' Silky said, her voice barely more than a whisper.

'Maybe there is,' Tallie declared, and his voice rang out more determined than they had ever heard. He turned to the fairies with tears in his eyes and spoke quickly, knowing he had very little time. 'Thank you for being my friends. I'll miss you all.' Then he grabbed the repaired Gemini Locket from Silky and bent low, looping the necklace around Talon's hand.

There was a flash and, when it faded, Tallie was gone. There was only Talon – still out cold – but with the Gemini Locket resting on his chest.

'What happened?' Bizzy asked.

'It was the Locket,' Silky answered. 'It can make doubles, but it can also bring them back together.'

'So Tallie's gone?' Bizzy asked.

'But the Land is recovering,' Petal responded. 'Look.'

Pinx, Bizzy and Silky followed Petal's gaze, taking in everything around them. Everywhere they looked, doubles danced in tandem and the Land thrived. The storm stopped, its dark clouds dissolving to reveal a sky filled with twin stars, decorating the sky with brilliant twin constellations. The cracked ground groaned back together, with new grass and double flowers growing over and erasing every seam. Twin full moons glowed high above and, illuminated by their light, a double rainbow arced across the night sky.

'It's *beautiful*,' Petal breathed in awe. 'Even the plants are singing and celebrating.'

But Pinx wasn't looking at the light show above. 'Want to see something really beautiful?' she asked admiringly. 'Look at that.'

Pinx nodded towards Melody and Mel, still dancing together. Their equally graceful bodies swirled, swooped and spun in perfect synchronicity – yet with subtle differences. Though they did the exact same motions, Melody's dance was gracefully controlled, while Mel's was energised with passion. Even after the Dance of the Doubles was complete, the twin Twinkletunes kept dancing, celebrating their kinship in a performance of

pure magic.

When they finally took one another's hands and bowed in a gracious finale, they seemed shocked to hear a roar of applause.

Everyone in Geminopolis had been awestruck watching them and they cheered and clapped until their voices were hoarse and their hands were sore. Melody blushed, embarrassed, but Mel loved it, and grinned as she waved her hands in the air, encouraging the ovation to go on and on.

When the applause finally died down, the moustached Ministers of Motion took their hands. 'Thank you,' they said, one gratefully and one with irritation.

'You're welcome,' Mel and Melody replied in unison, then laughed. 'But we should thank Tallie too,' Melody said. 'He reunited with Talon, even though he knew it would make him miserable.'

'Speaking of which,' Mel said, looking meaningfully at Melody. 'I suppose I should be going, too.'

Realising what she meant, Melody's eyes grew wide. 'What? No! You can't!'

Mel laughed. 'What am I supposed to do?
Keep you in this Land forever just so I can
exist on my own? Besides,' she added, her tone
turning serious. 'Now that we understand
each other, I don't really feel complete like
this. Do you?'

Melody thought about it, then shook her
head. 'No, I don't. We really do belong
together, don't we?'

'Yeah, we do,' Mel agreed. She turned to
the other fairies, who looked at her misty-
eyed, knowing what was coming next. 'Oh,
come on!' Mel laughed. 'You're not all going
soft on me, are you? And I expect more from
the likes of *you*,' she said, eyeing Pinx.

'Oh, I'm not crying,' Pinx said. 'It's Talon. I
can smell him from here and it's making my
eyes water.'

'Liar,' Mel grinned, and she and Pinx
grabbed each other in a huge hug. As they
separated, Mel whispered in her ear, 'Do me

one small favour and see what you can do with Melody's wardrobe, will you?'

'I promise,' Pinx whispered back.

'OK then,' Mel declared. 'So here goes everything.'

She plucked the Gemini Locket out of Talon's hand, then blew a kiss to Silky, Petal, Bizzy and Pinx. 'Goodbye!' she said. 'It's been a true honour to know you all.' Then she turned to Melody. 'Are you ready?'

'I suppose so,' Melody replied.

Locking eyes, Mel and Melody took a deep breath then Melody reached out for the Gemini Locket. The minute both doubles were touching it, the Locket flashed.

When the light had gone, Melody was alone. She seemed dazed and shook her head, blinking several times. The other fairies stared at her. Was she OK?

Melody cocked her head, a knowing smile dancing on her lips. 'What's the matter with you lot? Your eyes look like they're going to pop out of your face!'

'Mel?' Pinx asked.

But it was Melody's tinkling laughter that replied. 'No, it's me, Melody. But Mel's here too, in a way.'

Suddenly, Talon started to stir. 'We should go,' Silky said.

'Wait!' Pinx cried. 'His crystal! Let's take it with us!' She tried to reach for it, but every time her hand got close, it zipped away, as though it had a life of its own.

'It's a protection spell,' Bizzy said. 'I could try to break it, but it has to be incredibly strong to work when he's out cold like this . . .'

Silky shook her head. 'There's no time,' she said. 'We need to get the Gemini Locket back before Talon wakes up, and before the Land moves away from the Ladder.'

With the Talisman gone, Silky knew Talon wouldn't stick around the Land of Doubles, and she warned the Ministers of Motion to keep everyone out of his way until he left.

Since Melody still couldn't fly, Pinx, Petal, Silky and Bizzy worked together to support her weight, flying back to the Ladder as fast as they could and climbing down into the Faraway Tree just as the Land started to shift away.

Chapter Twelve
The Real Melody

The fairies were always excited to deliver their Talisman to Witch Whisper at the end of a mission, but they had never been so eager to tell her about their time in another Land before. They still couldn't get over Tallie, and they had been sure that Witch Whisper would be as stunned as they were to find that someone so sweet, kind and generous existed inside their worst enemy. But Witch Whisper never once gasped in shock at the story. She only nodded, a knowing smile on her face.

'OK, this is odd,' Pinx finally said. 'We're telling you there's someone wonderful inside the most hideous, horrible, disgusting creature in the history of disgusting creatures and you're not in the least bit surprised.'

Witch Whisper smiled. 'That's because I've seen the Tallie side of Talon before. We spent quite a lot of time together, long ago, and I've missed him very much. It's nice to hear that he's still alive in Talon, even if only in the smallest part.'

All five of the fairies' jaws dropped.

'Talon used to be like Tallie?'

'Back when you made the Talismans?'

'Was he like that all the time?'

'What happened?'

'When did he change?'

The fairies were dying for answers, but Witch Whisper assured them it was a *very* long story and one better saved for after a good night's sleep. After all, they had made it back to the Tree just as the Land moved away and there was no telling when a new Land and a new mission would arrive.

Reluctantly, the fairies agreed and, after Witch Whisper performed a spell to heal

Melody's wing, they flew back to their treehouse, all speculating about the strange history between Talon and Witch Whisper. They could have talked about the possibilities all night, but they were all tired and needed to get some rest.

Later that night, as Pinx was about to fall asleep, there was a gentle knock at her door.

'Hello?' she said sleepily.

Melody opened the door and flew in. 'Hi,' she said and, though it was clear she had something on her mind, she couldn't bring herself to meet Pinx's eyes.

'Melody?' Pinx asked, noticing her friend's discomfort. 'Is everything OK? Is your wing hurting again?'

'No, it's not that,' Melody said, 'Witch Whisper healed it perfectly.'

'Then what?'

Melody took a deep breath to steel herself, then flew over and sat on the edge of Pinx's bed. 'I just wanted to apologise,' she said softly.

'What for?' Pinx asked.

'For not being Mel,' she admitted. 'I know how much you loved her, and I'm guessing you're pretty disappointed. I mean, if only one of us were sticking around, I'm sure you'd have preferred it to be Mel, so . . . I'm sorry. That's all.'

Melody rose to leave, but Pinx caught her hand and stopped her, looking her deep in the eyes.

'I'm going to say something to you now and I want you to know I say it with the utmost love and respect . . . You have gone absolutely bonkers.'

'What?' Melody asked.

'Of course I loved Mel,' Pinx said. 'She was smart, she was funny, she spoke her mind, she definitely didn't suffer fools gladly, she had impeccable fashion taste –'

'I know!' Melody cried, tortured. 'That's

what I mean!'

'*But*,' Pinx cut her off, 'all the things I loved about Mel, well, those are the things I love about *you*. I see them all in there, even if you don't.'

Melody was stunned. 'You do?'

'I do. And I wouldn't trade you for anyone. Even Mel.'

Melody beamed, hugged her friend tightly and said goodnight. But before she left Pinx's room, she turned back.

'Um, Pinx? I actually really liked what you did with Mel's outfit, and the way she wore her hair. I don't know if I'd like to look that all the time, but . . . would you maybe give me one of your Faraway Tree Makeovers? You know, just to try it?'

Pinx leaped out of bed, now completely awake and excited. 'Are you *kidding*? I thought you'd never ask!'

Before Melody could even blink, Pinx was

at her side, pulling her into her room and gushing over all the amazing ways she'd transform her friend's wardrobe.

The two stayed up all night together, talking and laughing and having great fun experimenting with different looks for Melody.

It couldn't have been a more perfect night.

EGMONT PRESS: ETHICAL PUBLISHING

Egmont Press is about turning writers into successful authors and children into passionate readers – producing books that enrich and entertain. As a responsible children's publisher, we go even further, considering the world in which our consumers are growing up.

Safety First
Naturally, all of our books meet legal safety requirements. But we go further than this; every book with play value is tested to the highest standards – if it fails, it's back to the drawing-board.

Made Fairly
We are working to ensure that the workers involved in our supply chain – the people that make our books – are treated with fairness and respect.

Responsible Forestry
We are committed to ensuring all our papers come from environmentally and socially responsible forest sources.

**For more information, please visit our website at
www.egmont.co.uk/ethical**